CANDLEWICK PRESS
CAMBRIDGE, MASSACHUSETTS

Text copyright 1953 by Philip Booth. Copyright renewed © 1981 by Philip Booth. Illustrations copyright © 2001 by Bagram Ibatoulline. All rights reserved. No part of this book may be reproduced, transmitted, or stored in an information retrieval system in any form or by any means, graphic, electronic, or mechanical, including photocopying, taping, and recording, without prior written permission from the publisher. First edition 2001. "Crossing" from LETTER FROM A DISTANT LAND by Philip Booth. Published by arrangement with Viking Penguin, a division of Penguin Putnam Inc. Library of Congress Cataloging-in-Publication Data. Booth, Philip E. Crossing / Philip Booth ; illustrations by Bagram Ibatoulline. —1st ed. p. cm. ISBN 0-7636-1420-3 1. Railroads —Crossings—Juvenile poetry. 2. Children's poetry, American. [1. Railroads —Trains—Poetry. 2. American poetry.] I. Ibatoulline, Bagram, ill. II. Title PS3552.O647 C76 2001 811'.54—dc21 00-039781 Printed in Italy. This book was typeset in New Century Schoolbook. The illustrations were done in gouache. Candlewick Press, 2067 Massachusetts Avenue, Cambridge, Massachusetts 02140. Visit us at www.candlewick.com.

CROSSING

PHILIP BOOTH

illustrated by
BAGRAM IBATOULLINE

STOP   LOO

K LISTEN

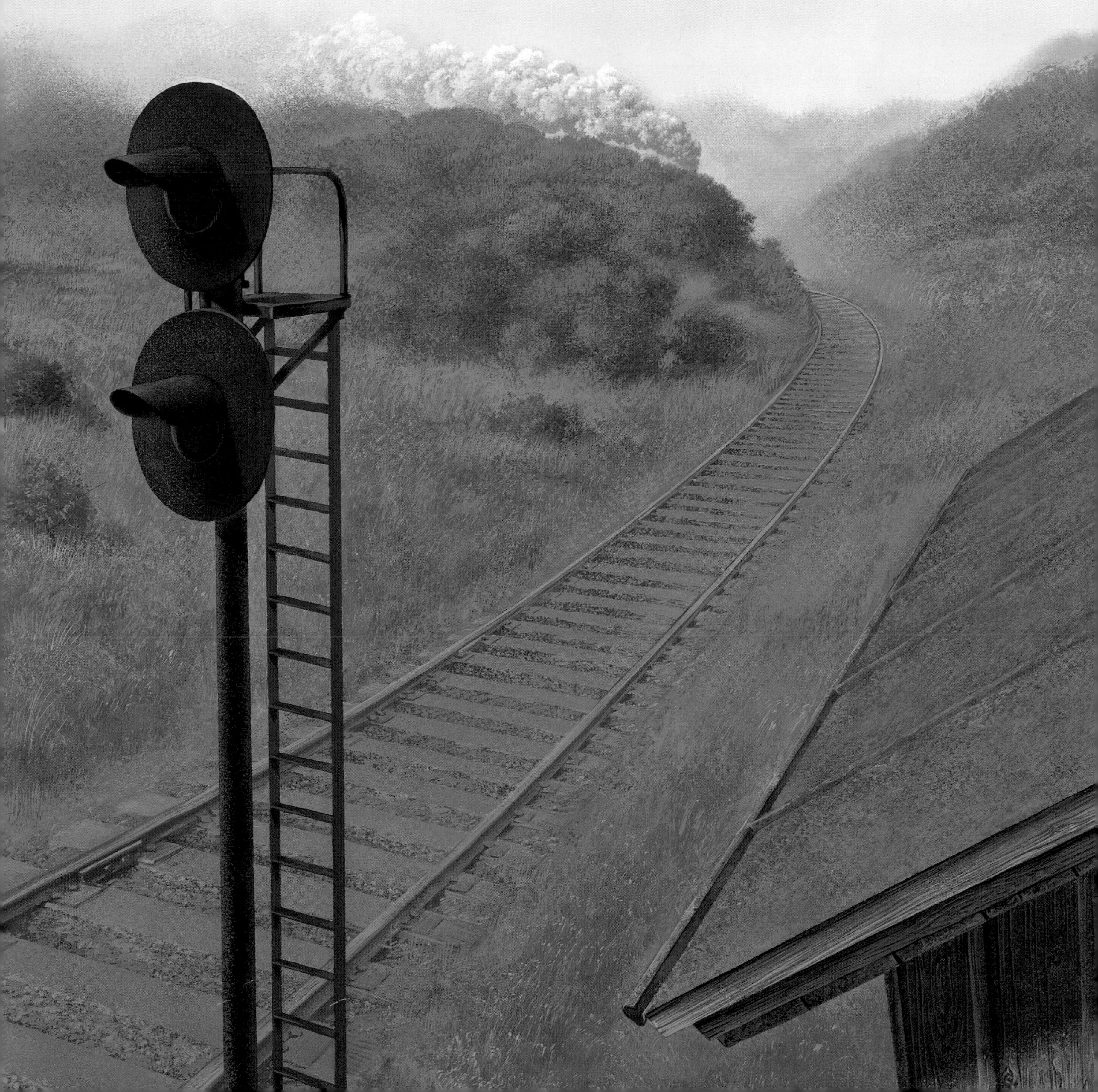

as gate stripes swing down,

count the cars hauling distance
upgrade through town:

warning whistle, bellclang,
engine eating steam,

engineer waving,
a fast-freight dream:

B&M boxcar,

boxcar again,

Frisco gondola,

eight-nine-ten,

Erie and Wabash,
Seaboard, U.P.,

Pennsy tankcar,
twenty-two, three,

Phoebe Snow, B&O,

thirty-four, five,

Santa Fe cattle
shipped alive,

red cars, yellow cars,

orange cars, black,

Youngstown steel
down to Mobile

on Rock Island track,

fifty-nine, sixty,
hoppers of coke,

Anaconda copper,
hotbox smoke,

eighty-eight,
red-ball freight,

Rio Grande,
Nickel Plate,

Hiawatha,
Lackawanna,

rolling fast
and loose,

ninety-seven,
coal car,

boxcar,

CABOOSE!